To my unique family of bookworms,
who inspired and encouraged me to believe in my stories —J.F.

To the Early Bird —D.E.S.

 Published in the United States by Anne Schwartz Books,
an imprint of Random House Children's Books, a division of Penguin Random House LLC, New York.
Anne Schwartz Books and the colophon are trademarks of Penguin Random House LLC.

Visit us on the Web! rhcbooks.com
Educators and librarians, for a variety of teaching tools, visit us at RHTeachersLibrarians.com

Library of Congress Cataloging-in-Publication Data is available upon request.
ISBN 978-0-593-12478-9 (trade) — ISBN 978-0-593-12479-6 (lib. bdg.) — ISBN 978-0-593-12480-2 (ebook)

The text of this book is set in 15.75-point Archer.
The illustrations were created with ballpoint pen, photocopy,
watercolor, toothbrush, and Crayola airbrush.
Book design by Rachael Cole

MANUFACTURED IN CHINA
10 9 8 7 6 5 4 3 2 1
First Edition

THE WORM FAMILY HAS ITS PICTURE TAKEN

Caldecott Honoree
JENNIFER FRANK & DAVID EZRA STEIN

a·s·b
anne schwartz books

Mrs. Worm lay at the top of a giant dirt pile watching her children play. They were wriggling their bodies into all kinds of delightful shapes. She hoped she'd always remember how squirmy, slimy, and cute they were at this age, but she did not have a very good memory because her brain was so tiny.

"I know!" she declared. "I'll have our picture taken!"

The very next day Mrs. Worm called Mr. Muskrat, the photographer, to arrange a time.

Then she told her family.

“That is so COOL!” the oldest, Emma, exclaimed. She loved the idea of being able to see herself hanging on the wall every day.

Emma could hardly wait to tell her friend Ellie.

"How SPLENIDFEROUS!" squealed Ellie.

“We had our picture taken last year, and it was amazing. We had the most beautiful smiles.”

“Cool,” said Emma.

But then she thought about how worms don’t have teeth. How would they have beautiful smiles in their picture?

Oh, well, she decided. *We will still have a nice way to remember our family.*

On her way home, Emma bumped into her friend Abigail and told her about the family portrait.

“Too FABULOUS!” meowed Abigail.

“I just love having my picture taken. My human always takes me to the beauty salon first, so that my big poufy hair will look especially gorgeous.”

“Cool,” said Emma.

But then she thought about how worms don’t have hair. How could they look poufy and gorgeous in their picture?

Oh, well, she decided. *We will still have a nice way to remember our family.*

As she continued on her way, Emma was feeling a bit less excited. At the forsythia bush, she saw her friend Olivia sitting on a branch. Emma told her about the portrait.

"Ooooh! WOWEE!" squeaked Olivia, and flitted high above Emma's head. "My family took one of those just last week, and all our colors made it look like a rainbow!"

“Cool,” said Emma sadly as Olivia fluttered away on the breeze. She was already thinking about how worms are just one color. Her family was beautiful—she knew they were—but there would be no bright colors in their picture.

Oh, well, she decided. *We will still have a nice way to remember our family.*

But the rest of the trip home, Emma
couldn't help feeling much less excited.

As Emma fell asleep that night, she thought about what her friends had said.

How was her family going to make *their* portrait special?

When she woke up, she had an idea!

The day of the photo shoot arrived,
and Emma had a surprise for everyone.

"Preeeettyyy!" her little sisters squealed excitedly.

Mr. and Mrs. Worm were less sure.

Their new look was not comfortable.

Even though the Worm family arrived at the studio on time, Mr. Muskrat would not take their picture.

“I am sorry,” he said. “I have an appointment with a family of worms. You will have to come back another day.”

“But we *are* the family of worms,” said Mrs. Worm.

The photographer laughed. "For one thing, worms do not have teeth," he said.

Mrs. Worm quickly instructed her family to spit out their fake teeth.

“And they do not have hair,” said Mr. Muskrat.

The family took off their wigs.

“And they most definitely are not colorful.”

The family undressed. “AHHHHHHHH . . . ,” they all said.

"Oh!" said Mr. Muskrat, looking very surprised.
"I am terribly sorry I didn't recognize you."

Then together, the Worm family wriggled and squiggled and squeezed into a delightful pose only a worm family could make.

Mr. Muskrat snapped the picture. The first of their many annual portraits was taken.

Cheese
Muskrat

The next morning Emma sat with her family, admiring the portrait now hanging in their worm hideaway. "It's perfectly PERFECT!" she whispered.

And she would have reached out and given them a great big hug . . . if she'd had arms.